Book 9
by every
them

PUMPKIN MYSTERY

By Tammi Salzano
Illustrated by Duendes del Sur

ISBN 978-0-545-35547-6

12 11 10 9 8 7 6 5 4 3                                      12 13 14 15/0
                                                                    95
Printed in China
First printing, October 2011

# SCHOLASTIC INC.

New York   Toronto   London   Auckland
Sydney   Mexico City   New Delhi   Hong Kong

Scooby and his friends are picking pumpkins.
They walk **by** the pumpkin patch.
Look at all of **them**!

They carry pumpkins.
They put **them by** the van.
Look at all of **them**!

Scooby and Shaggy explore.
They run **by** a scarecrow.
The scarecrow scares **them**!

Scooby and Shaggy
stop **by** the van.
Ruh-roh!
**Every** pumpkin is gone!
Who took **them**?
Did the scarecrow
take **them**?

Scooby and Shaggy run **by** Velma. They tell her **every** pumpkin is gone. They tell her the scarecrow took **them**.

Scooby and Shaggy run **by** Fred.
They tell him **every** pumpkin is gone.
They tell him the scarecrow took **them**.

Scooby and Shaggy
run **by** Daphne.
They tell her **every**
pumpkin is gone.
They tell her the
scarecrow took **them**.

Here is **every** pumpkin!
They used **them** to make
food. Rummy!